DINOSAUR COVE™

SAVING THE SCALY BEAST

by
REX STONE

illustrated by
MIKE SPOOR

Series created by
Working Partners Ltd

OXFORD
UNIVERSITY PRESS

Special thanks to Jane Clarke.

To Helen and Amy, with love. R.S.

For Hannah, Alice and Imogen. M.S.

OXFORD
UNIVERSITY PRESS

Great Clarendon Street, Oxford OX2 6DP
Oxford University Press is a department of the University of Oxford.
It furthers the University's objective of excellence in research, scholarship,
and education by publishing worldwide in

Oxford   New York

Auckland   Cape Town   Dar es Salaam   Hong Kong   Karachi
Kuala Lumpur   Madrid   Melbourne   Mexico City   Nairobi
New Delhi   Shanghai   Taipei   Toronto

With offices in

Argentina   Austria   Brazil   Chile   Czech Republic   France   Greece
Guatemala   Hungary   Italy   Japan   Poland   Portugal   Singapore
South Korea   Switzerland   Thailand   Turkey   Ukraine   Vietnam

Oxford is a registered trade mark of Oxford University Press
in the UK and in certain other countries

British Library Cataloguing in Publication Data

Data available

ISBN: 978-0-19-275630-5

3 5 7 9 10 8 6 4

Printed in Great Britain
Paper used in the production of this book is a natural,
recyclable product made from wood grown in sustainable forests
The manufacturing process conforms to the environmental
regulations of the country of origin

FACT FILE

➡ JAMIE AND HIS BEST FRIEND, TOM, HAVE A SECRET—THEY'VE DISCOVERED A CAVE THAT LEADS THE WAY TO DINO WORLD! IF THE BOYS PLACE THEIR FEET INTO A SET OF FOSSILIZED DINOSAUR PRINTS THEY'RE INSTANTLY TRANSPORTED TO AN ANCIENT LAND OF PREHISTORIC BEASTS. IN THE PERMIAN ERA, THE BOYS GO ADVENTURING IN THE JUNGLE. BUT THEY QUICKLY DISCOVER THAT THERE'S MORE AMONGST THE VINES THAN JUST BUGS.

JAMIE

- **FULL NAME:** JAMIE MORGAN
- **AGE:** 8 YEARS
- **SIZE:** 1 JATOM*
- **TOP SPEED:** 10 KPH
- **LIKES:** FOSSIL HUNTING AND LEARNING ABOUT DINOSAURS
- **DISLIKES:** BEING STUCK INDOORS

Jamie's eye

Jamie's foot

Jamie's hand

*NOTE A JATOM IS THE SIZE OF JAMIE OR TOM: 125 CM TALL AND 27 KG IN WEIGHT

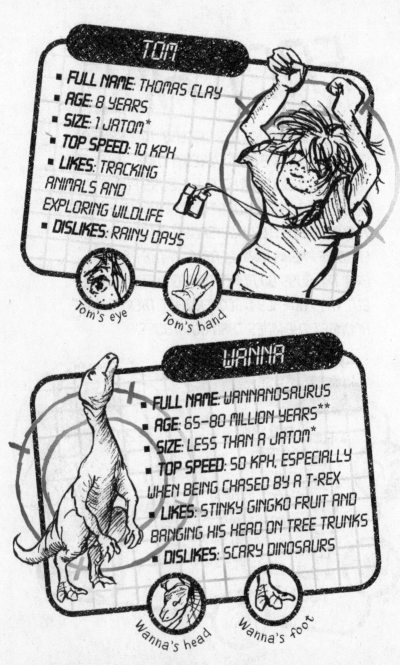

TOM

- **FULL NAME:** THOMAS CLAY
- **AGE:** 8 YEARS
- **SIZE:** 1 JATOM*
- **TOP SPEED:** 10 KPH
- **LIKES:** TRACKING ANIMALS AND EXPLORING WILDLIFE
- **DISLIKES:** RAINY DAYS

Tom's eye

Tom's hand

WANNA

- **FULL NAME:** WANNANOSAURUS
- **AGE:** 65-80 MILLION YEARS**
- **SIZE:** LESS THAN A JATOM*
- **TOP SPEED:** 50 KPH, ESPECIALLY WHEN BEING CHASED BY A T-REX
- **LIKES:** STINKY GINGKO FRUIT AND BANGING HIS HEAD ON TREE TRUNKS
- **DISLIKES:** SCARY DINOSAURS

Wanna's head

Wanna's foot

*NOTE: A JATOM IS THE SIZE OF JAMIE OR TOM: 125 CM TALL AND 27 KG IN WEIGHT
**NOTE: SCIENTISTS CALL THIS PERIOD THE LATE CRETACEOUS

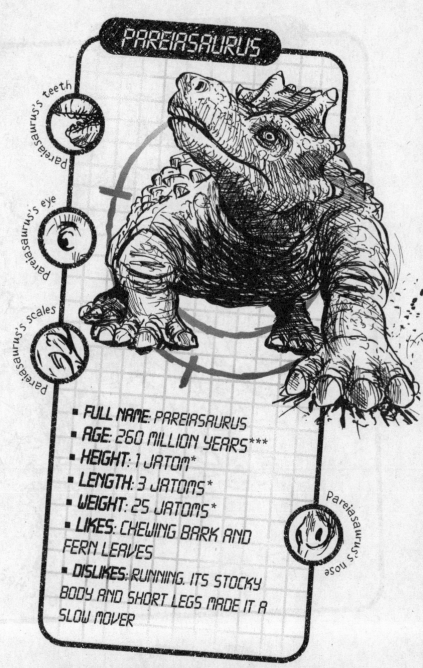

PAREIASAURUS

pareiasaurus's teeth

pareiasaurus's eye

pareiasaurus's scales

pareiasaurus's nose

- **FULL NAME:** PAREIASAURUS
- **AGE:** 260 MILLION YEARS***
- **HEIGHT:** 1 JATOM*
- **LENGTH:** 3 JATOMS*
- **WEIGHT:** 25 JATOMS*
- **LIKES:** CHEWING BARK AND FERN LEAVES
- **DISLIKES:** RUNNING. ITS STOCKY BODY AND SHORT LEGS MADE IT A SLOW MOVER

*NOTE: A JATOM IS THE SIZE OF JAMIE OR TOM: 125 CM TALL AND 27 KG IN WEIGHT
***NOTE: SCIENTISTS CALL THIS PERIOD THE PERMIAN

DINOSAUR COVE

Village

Marina

Sealight Head

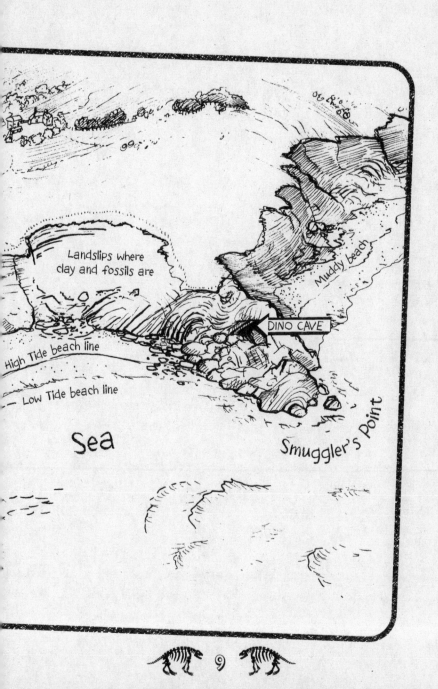

Landslips where
clay and fossils are

Muddy beach

DINO CAVE

High Tide beach line

Low Tide beach line

Sea

Smuggler's Point

CHAPTER 1

SEARCH:

A great crash came from the basement of the old lighthouse in Dinosaur Cove.

'Stop!' Jamie Morgan warned. His best friend Tom Clay froze, about to open the door.

Jamie's dad had sent the boys to the basement to collect a box of replica early human clothing and equipment for an Ice Age display in his dinosaur museum. But something was in there. The boys pressed their ears to the door and listened to the scritch-scratching noise it was making.

Tom looked at Jamie. 'That's the sound of claws.'

'Like something from Dino World,' Jamie agreed. They'd met dinosaurs and prehistoric beasts with vicious claws in the secret world they'd discovered in the Cove.

'Maybe it's that inostrancevia that keeps hunting us,' Tom joked nervously, remembering the bear-like creature they had met the last time they visited Dino World.

There was a clattering noise and a loud screech.

Meooooow!

'It's not a dinosaur, it's a cat-o-saur!' Jamie cracked open the door

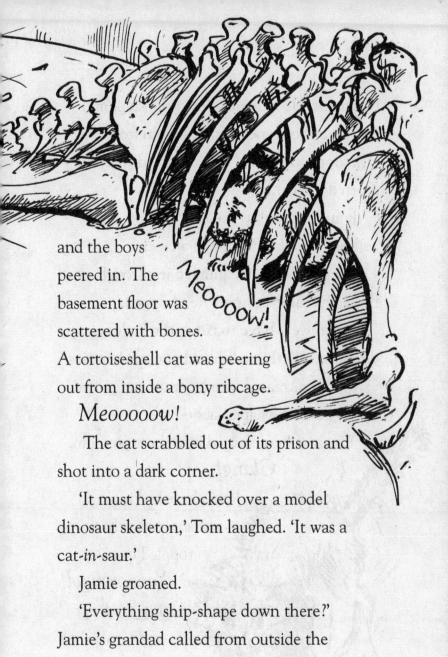

and the boys peered in. The basement floor was scattered with bones. A tortoiseshell cat was peering out from inside a bony ribcage.

Meooooow!

The cat scrabbled out of its prison and shot into a dark corner.

'It must have knocked over a model dinosaur skeleton,' Tom laughed. 'It was a cat-*in*-saur.'

Jamie groaned.

'Everything ship-shape down there?' Jamie's grandad called from outside the basement. He clomped down the steps and surveyed the scene. 'That's Pippin from the farm down the road,' he exclaimed when he spotted the cat.

Jamie pointed to the tiny window at ceiling level that was open a crack.

'Pippin must have jumped in through there,' he said, 'but now he's trapped.'

'Then we'll have to catch the little scamp,' Grandad told them. 'Spread out, me hearties.'

Pippin retreated into a corner and puffed up his fur as they approached.

Tom and Jamie edged into the storeroom.

Clang!

Jamie knocked into a rusty spade, that toppled over.

Yeooowwwl!

Pippin leapt up onto a shelf

in alarm, dislodging one
of the boxes.

Thunk!

The box fell to the floor. Leather shoes, a
bow and arrows and what looked like a wooden
tennis racket came tumbling out. A feather
detached itself from the end of one of the
arrows and floated to the floor by Tom's feet.

'That's the box Dad sent us to find,' Jamie
remarked. 'Looks like they played tennis in
the Ice Age!'

'It's a snowshoe, you wombat,' Tom
snorted. 'You strap them to your feet to stop
you from sinking in deep snow.'

'I was joking. I knew that!' Jamie retorted.

Hisss!

Pippin spat as he looked down
at them, bristling
from nose
to tail.

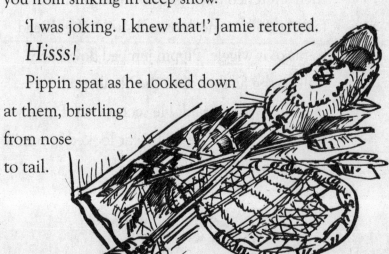

'We're scaring him,' Jamie murmured. 'How are we going to get him down without getting clawed?'

Tom picked up the feather that had fallen from the arrow. 'Cats love to play,' he said.

An old red tartan blanket was draped over the antlers of a moth-eaten moose head. Tom pulled a thread loose from it, then tied the feather to one end and set the blanket down on the floor.

'Here, Pippin.' Tom dangled the feather in front of the frightened cat. Pippin looked at it suspiciously for a moment, then stretched out a paw to pat it. Tom let the feather drift to the floor and shook the thread to make it wiggle. Pippin jumped down and stalked the feather onto the blanket.

'Neat!' Jamie said. He scooped up Pippin in the tartan blanket. The cat looked at him in surprise, then began to purr.

16

'Well done, lads,'
Grandad told them.
'You two get Pippin back
home while I clear up.'

Purr

'If we're quick, we'll
have time to go to Dino
World!' Jamie whispered,
handing Pippin, still snuggled in the blanket, to
Tom. He dashed upstairs, grabbed his backpack,
and joined Tom outside. They jogged along the
road towards the old stone farmhouse.

As soon as Pippin spotted it coming into
view, he mewed in delight, leapt out of Tom's
arms and shot off home.

Jamie stuffed the empty blanket in his
backpack.

'Hurry up.' Tom hopped impatiently from
foot to foot. 'Wanna's waiting for us.'

Jamie grinned from ear to ear. He couldn't
wait to see their little dino friend again.

The boys raced to the beach, scrambled up the rocks, and squeezed into their secret cave.

'Dino World, here we come,' Jamie panted. His heart thumped with excitement as he fitted his feet into the line of fossilized dinosaur footprints and stepped towards the rock face. Tom was close behind him.

'One . . . two . . . three . . . four . . . FIVE!'

There was a lightning-like flash and Tom and Jamie zapped 265 million years back in time into the dark, dusty cave that was their entry point to the Permian age.

'There's Wanna,' Tom cried. He pointed up the tunnel leading out of the cave. Their dino friend's scales were shining in the sunshine and his tail was wagging so hard that it was a blur. As the boys scrambled out into the sizzling heat, the little wannanosaurus greeted them with a playful butt of his bony head.

'Ooof!' Jamie exclaimed, doubling over. It felt as if all the air had been knocked out of him. Wanna stuck his nose into Jamie's backpack, sniffed the blanket and sneezed.

Atchooo!

'You're the first dino ever to smell a cat,' Jamie laughed. But Tom had his finger to his lips and was looking worried.

Garrr!

A faint but familiar roar came from the gritty red slopes of the volcano in the distance. Wanna looked up and grunked softly.

'The inostie's hanging around again,' Tom said, scanning the steep rocks with his binoculars. 'I can't see it, though . . . '

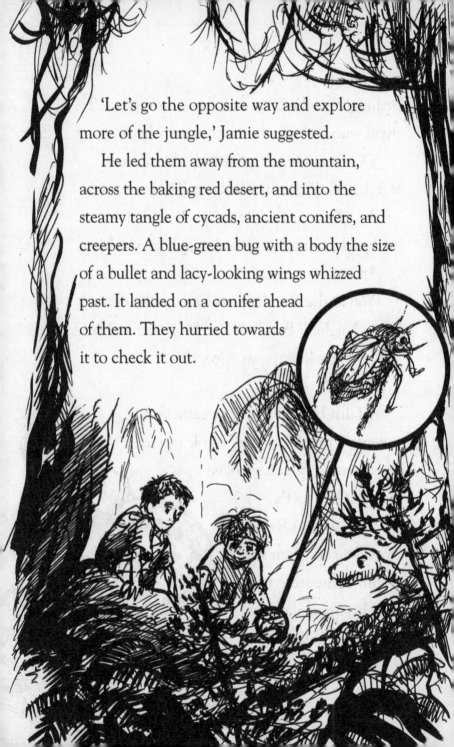

'Let's go the opposite way and explore more of the jungle,' Jamie suggested.

He led them away from the mountain, across the baking red desert, and into the steamy tangle of cycads, ancient conifers, and creepers. A blue-green bug with a body the size of a bullet and lacy-looking wings whizzed past. It landed on a conifer ahead of them. They hurried towards it to check it out.

'Awesome bu— ' Jamie didn't get to
finish his sentence. He yelped as the ground
vanished under his feet.

Thump!

Jamie, Tom, and Wanna landed in the
soft leaf mould at the bottom of a huge hole.
Jamie glanced around in dismay. The sides of
the pit were steep and crumbly-looking. They
were trapped!

Wanna looked up and tipped his head to
one side, listening intently. Tom and Jamie
strained their ears. Something was snorting
and snuffling towards them.
The sides of the pit began
to shudder and a shadow
blotted out the sun.

'If that's a
predator,' Tom
gasped, 'we're
its dinner!'

CHAPTER 2

SEARCH:

A huge reptilian head loomed above them.
It bent its turtle-like neck and peered over
the edge of the pit. Its open mouth was full
of big flat teeth. Jamie's knees were knocking
with fear. He had a close-up view of every
rubbery yellow scale that lined the creature's
thick neck.

*Any minute now, we'll be going down that
throat,* he thought.

The creature sniffed and lowered its great
head towards them. Its muzzle was striped

with lines of green scales. Jamie thought it looked vaguely familiar.

Wanna's tail began to wag.

Grunk, grunk, grunk!

'It's that pareiasaurus we met last time!' Tom breathed a sigh of relief. 'We checked it out on the Fossil Finder. It's a herbivore, not a meat eater.'

As if in agreement, the parry blinked and gave a friendly moo.

'Phew!' The boys looked at each other and laughed. It was safe to get out.

'I'll give you a leg up,' Tom said.

He cupped his hands together so that Jamie could fit his foot into them, then he boosted his friend up. Jamie heaved himself out of the hole, showering leaf mould down on Tom.

'Get me out of here before you bury me,' Tom complained, shaking leaves from his hair.

25

Jamie bent down and stretched out his hand, helping Tom haul himself out.

From inside the pit, Wanna looked up at them, grunking pathetically.

Mooooooooo!

The parry lowed in sympathy.

Jamie leaned down again. 'I can't reach Wanna's front legs. They're too short to grab,' he groaned. 'We should have got him out first.' He lay on his tummy and poked his head over the pit. 'Hang on to my ankles,' he told Tom. 'Now, lower me over the edge until my head's level with Wanna's. That's it . . .'

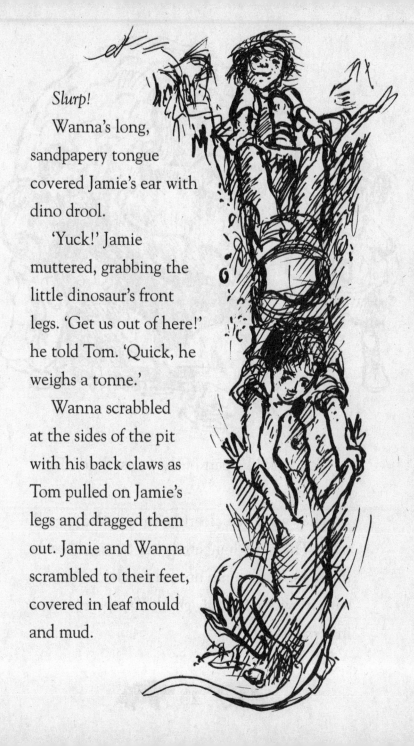

Slurp!

Wanna's long, sandpapery tongue covered Jamie's ear with dino drool.

'Yuck!' Jamie muttered, grabbing the little dinosaur's front legs. 'Get us out of here!' he told Tom. 'Quick, he weighs a tonne.'

Wanna scrabbled at the sides of the pit with his back claws as Tom pulled on Jamie's legs and dragged them out. Jamie and Wanna scrambled to their feet, covered in leaf mould and mud.

'You look like part of the forest floor,' Tom chuckled.

They were in a clearing, surrounded by tall trees. The parry lumbered over to stand beside the boys. Wanna ran up and touched noses with it, with a friendly *grunk*. The parry lowed in response.

'Aw,' Tom murmured. 'They're friends now.'

'I'm glad Wanna's friend didn't fall down the hole,' Jamie said. 'We'd never have got it out. It looks as big and heavy as a baby elephant.'

'And as friendly as one, too,' Tom smiled, scratching the thick, knobbly skin behind the parry's ears.

Jamie patted it on the back, feeling the bony bumps along its spine. The parry made a low rumble at the back of its throat.

'It's purring like Pippin,' Jamie laughed.

All of a sudden, Wanna clambered onto an old tree trunk that lay with its thickest end close to the edge of the pit. He stuck his nose into the air and sniffed deeply.

Gak! Gak! Gak!

The parry stopped purring and froze.

Tom and Jamie followed the direction Wanna's nose was pointing. The ferns at the edge of the trees were rustling as if they were being blown by the breeze.

But there was no wind—the air in the clearing was hot and still. The boys looked at each other in alarm.

Eooowww!

The loud screech echoed round the clearing. Jamie, Tom, and Wanna leapt behind the fallen tree trunk and peeped over the top of it as a hunched-over crocodile-like creature stalked out of the ferns.

Its beady eyes were
fixed on the parry
left standing in
the clearing.
Drool was
dripping
from the

sabre-like fangs that hung over its
powerful lower jaw.

Jamie recognized it from the Fossil
Finder's list of Permian predators.
'Anteosaurus,' he breathed.

The creature was the size of a minibus, bright green, with speckles of darker green on its back. It blended in perfectly with the young sun-dappled ferns behind it.

They watched from behind the tree trunk as the parry pulled its head into the folds of its knobbly neck.

'Like a turtle or a tortoise does,' Tom murmured. 'But it doesn't have a shell strong enough to protect it from those fangs . . .'

Eooowwww!

The anteo lunged at the parry. Just in time, the parry lumbered round so its back was facing the anteo, and lashed it away with its tail.

The anteo made a hissing noise and gnashed its teeth. It circled round the parry until the two creatures were standing face-to-face once more. The anteo crouched over, swishing its own crocodilian tail. The boys could see the muscles in its powerful legs

quivering as it prepared
to pounce.

'The parry doesn't stand a chance,' Jamie
cried. 'We have to do something!'

EOOOWWWW!

CHAPTER 3

The anteosaurus twitched its tail, like a scaly giant cat about to spring.

Quick as a flash, Tom grabbed the tartan blanket from Jamie's backpack and leapt out from the cover of the fallen log. He hurled the blanket over the anteo's eyes as it launched itself towards the parry.

Eooowww!

The anteo screamed, furiously shaking its head and snapping its great teeth. The thick blanket was firmly hooked on the rough scales

on its head and was flapping over its beady eyes. The ferocious predator backed away into the forest. The boys could hear it growling and thrashing in the ferns as it tried to shake off the blanket.

The parry looked anxiously in the direction of the anteo as Jamie and Wanna stepped out from their hiding place.

'It'll soon free itself,' Tom warned. 'We have to get the parry out of here.'

'An anteo can easily outrun a parry,' Jamie said. 'We have to buy it more time to get away. But how?'

Wanna ran back towards the pit.

Grunk!

The little dino peered over the edge.

Grunk, Grunk!

'Wanna's got it!' Jamie exclaimed. 'We can trap the anteo in the pit. That'll slow it down.'

'It's closer to the ground than we are,' Tom retorted. 'It'll see the hole.'

'Not if we cover it in ferns,' Jamie told him.

'But the hole's too big, the ferns will fall in . . . ' Tom looked round wildly.

Jamie hauled a creeper down from the closest tree. 'We can make a criss-cross grid to hold up the ferns,' he explained breathlessly, weighing one end of the creeper down at the edge of the pit with a rock.

Tom ran to the opposite side of the pit. Jamie lobbed the other end of the creeper to him and Tom secured it with a heavy stone. Three creepers later, and the pit was covered with a grid of vines.

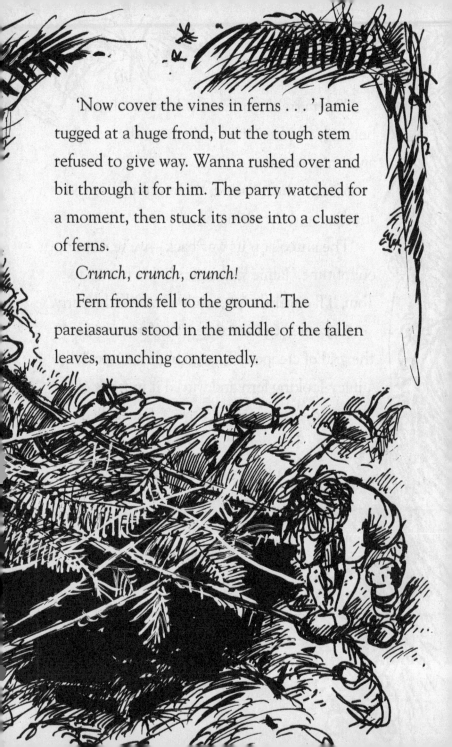

'Now cover the vines in ferns . . . ' Jamie tugged at a huge frond, but the tough stem refused to give way. Wanna rushed over and bit through it for him. The parry watched for a moment, then stuck its nose into a cluster of ferns.

Crunch, crunch, crunch!

Fern fronds fell to the ground. The pareiasaurus stood in the middle of the fallen leaves, munching contentedly.

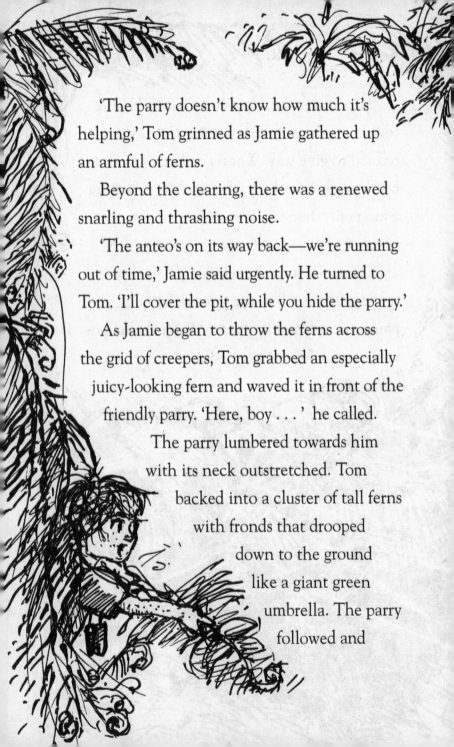

'The parry doesn't know how much it's helping,' Tom grinned as Jamie gathered up an armful of ferns.

Beyond the clearing, there was a renewed snarling and thrashing noise.

'The anteo's on its way back—we're running out of time,' Jamie said urgently. He turned to Tom. 'I'll cover the pit, while you hide the parry.'

As Jamie began to throw the ferns across the grid of creepers, Tom grabbed an especially juicy-looking fern and waved it in front of the friendly parry. 'Here, boy . . . ' he called.

The parry lumbered towards him with its neck outstretched. Tom backed into a cluster of tall ferns with fronds that drooped down to the ground like a giant green umbrella. The parry followed and

Wanna squeezed in after them. The little dino
stood next to the parry as if he was on guard.
The two dinosaurs were almost totally hidden
from view.

Tom dashed back to Jamie.

'Awesome!' he exclaimed. 'I can't see the
pit at all now. What's the bait to get the anteo
into the trap?'

Eeeooowww!

The anteo stalked into the clearing, trailing the shredded blanket from its shoulders like a cloak. It fixed its beady eyes on Jamie and Tom.

'Run!' Jamie and Tom raced round to the far side of the pit.

'So we're the bait . . . ' Tom said, panting next to Jamie. 'Not one of your better ideas, fossil brain . . . '

The anteo raised its nose to the air and sniffed. It slunk slowly towards the boys, like a cat stalking a mouse.

'It's working,' Jamie whispered triumphantly. 'When it charges at us, it'll fall into the pit.'

Mooooo!

But there was a snort of alarm from the umbrella of ferns.

'The parry!' Tom gasped.
'If it doesn't keep quiet, the
anteo's going to charge it
instead of us!'

The anteo took a few
paces towards the noise. It
sniffed deeply and growled.

Eooowww!

'Not there,
here!' Jamie
shouted. He and Tom jumped
up and down, desperately
waving their arms to make the
anteo charge at them.

The anteo hunched its body,
ready to pounce. Its tail swished.

'It's too far away from the pit now,' Jamie
gasped. 'It's going to miss . . .'

'. . . and get us!' Tom groaned as the
ferocious predator launched into its spring.

43

Gak!

Wanna leapt from the cover of the ferns with his head held low.

Thwack!

His bony skull hit the anteo and it tumbled sideways into the pit. There was a loud *crash* and an outraged roar.

'Well done, Wanna!' Jamie cheered.

Jamie, Tom, Wanna, and the parry peered nervously down into the pit. The anteo was wriggling around in a tangle of ferns and vines. It struggled to its feet and stood on its hind legs, hissing and spitting with rage as it scrabbled at the sides.

'It's stuck for now,' Jamie confirmed. 'Let's get the parry to safety before it escapes.'

Tom plucked a handful of fresh young fern fronds and waved them under the parry's nose.

'This way!' he ordered, luring it into the trees. Jamie and Wanna followed behind.

44

'The anteo could track us when it gets out,'
Tom said as he led them deep into the jungle.
'We need to cross a stream or
something to cover up
our scent.'

'The ground's getting spongier,' Jamie commented. 'Look!' He pointed to a shimmering line of sunlight glinting off what looked like wet ground.

They hurried towards it. Then, without any warning, Tom and the parry stopped so suddenly that Jamie and Wanna bumped into the back of them. They were standing at the edge of a wide oozy river of mud.

'There's no way round,' Tom muttered.

Jamie prodded the thick shiny mud with his foot.

'I reckon it will hold my weight,' he said, taking a cautious step. Wanna did the same, and Tom.

'The parry will be safe on the other side of this mud,' Tom said jubilantly. 'The anteo will never be able to cross it, it's too heavy.' He waved the ferns at the parry again.

Mooo!

The parry took a cautious step onto the mud. For a moment, it looked as if the mud would support its weight, but then slowly, very slowly, its foot began to sink.

Jamie's heart sank, too.

'The parry's too heavy,' he groaned as the friendly creature pulled its sturdy front leg out of the ooze and backed away. 'How can it reach the other side without getting stuck in the mud?'

CHAPTER 4

The parry turned away from the river of mud
and began to nibble at the bark of a nearby
conifer.

'Maybe there is a way to stop it sinking,'
Jamie said. 'Snowshoes!'

'You're crackers,' Tom told him. 'We'll have
to wait more than a hundred million years for
it to snow around here and freeze the mud.'

'I know that, you wombat,' Jamie said
excitedly. 'Remember the snowshoes in the
museum basement? They work because they

spread a person's weight over a bigger surface and stop them sinking . . .'

'I get it,' Tom grinned. 'We make snowshoes for a pareiasaurus. But how?'

The boys glanced around. Behind them, the parry had stripped the tough outer layer from the trunk of the conifer and was standing in a heap of bark, mooing contentedly to itself as it chewed.

Moo!

Tom and Jamie looked at each other.

Tom grabbed a piece of bark and tested it in his hands. 'It's strong enough,' he said, rolling a long piece into a tube.

Jamie rolled another piece and bent it into a curve. 'And bendy enough,' he added. 'There's plenty of stuff to tie it together.' He reached up and pulled a vine from the tree.

Wanna watched as Tom and Jamie lashed pieces of bark together with the tough thin vines that dangled from branches. Soon they had four

51

strong tyre-sized
discs with long vine
shoelaces dangling
from them.

Tom coaxed the parry to the
edge of the mud once more. He gently patted
one of the parry's back legs. The parry made a
rumbling purr, but stood rooted to the spot.

'We have to get it to lift its leg,' Tom
told Jamie.

Wanna put his head to one side and
watched as the boys heaved and tugged at
the parry's pillar-like back leg. The friendly
creature looked at them curiously and purred
to itself, but it didn't budge.

Grunk!

Wanna lowered his bony head and gently
barged into the parry's knee.

The parry glanced down in surprise and
lifted its foot.

'Great work, Wanna,' Jamie commented.

Tom quickly placed the bark shoe on the ground beneath the parry's foot, taking care to spread out the laces before it landed again. Jamie used the shoelace vines to tie the shoe to the parry's scaly foot, making a big bow just behind the creature's mud-filled toenails.

With Wanna's help, the bark shoes were soon strapped to all four of the pareiasaurus's feet. Tom chuckled as he, Jamie, and Wanna led the way onto the mud.

'It looks like a dino-puppy with feet that are much too big for its body,' he said. Tom held some chewy bark in front of the parry's nose. It stretched out its neck and stepped cautiously onto the mud.

'It's working!' Jamie cheered as, step by step, they coaxed the parry across the gloopy mud.

It left a trail of
great tyre-sized
prints.

'If those prints get
fossilized, scientists will think
they've discovered a giant new species
living in the Permian,' Tom said.

They reached the other side of the mud
and Tom untied the vine lacings from the

parry's feet. The creature spotted a cluster of
young ferns and lumbered happily towards it.

Scrunch!

It took a great mouthful.

'Your friend's safe from that anteo now,'
Jamie told Wanna.

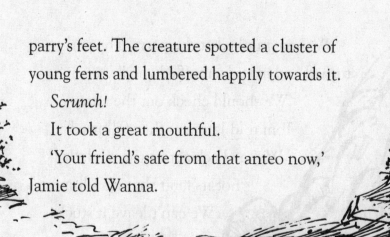

Wanna grunked at the parry. The parry
turned and *mooed* a muffled goodbye.

'We should check out the anteo,'
Tom told Jamie as they followed
Wanna back across the mud. 'It's
not its fault that it's a hunter.
We can't leave it stuck
in that pit.'

'It might die
of hunger if
it can't
get out,'
Jamie
agreed.
A ferocious
growling and
hissing noise was
coming from the
pit. They approached
cautiously.

'There's the blanket!' Tom whispered, pointing out the tattered remains lying on the fallen tree trunk. 'It must have caught on the bark when the anteo fell in.'

Wanna sniffed at the blanket and sneezed.

'We'll have a tough time explaining this to Grandad,' Jamie commented as he stuffed the shredded blanket into his backpack.

Wanna peered into the pit, and immediately leapt back behind Tom and Jamie. The boys nervously looked over the edge. The anteo was gnashing its teeth and foaming at the mouth. When it caught sight of the boys, it started hurling itself at the sides of the pit.

Eooooowww!

'Scary,' Jamie said with a shudder. 'You sure it's a good idea to get it out?'

Tom made his fist into an imaginary microphone.

'This is Tom Clay reporting from the Permian, where a giant and very ferocious anteosaur is trapped in a pit,' he commentated nervously. 'Our task is to rescue it. But it's going to be very tricky getting it out without being eaten!'

CHAPTER 5

'So, how do we get a prehistoric predator out of a pit?' Jamie demanded.

Tom pointed to the fallen tree trunk. It was covered in knobbly bumps where branches had broken off.

'If we tip that into the hole, the anteo can climb up it. It has plenty of footholds,' he told Jamie.

'But the anteo will pounce on us and eat us if we're still holding on to the end.' Jamie sounded unconvinced.

'Not if we use vines to drag it into the pit,' Tom explained. 'If we make some extra-long ropes, we'll have a head start to get away.'

'That might work,' Jamie agreed.

Wanna watched curiously as the boys pulled vines from the trees and knotted them together to make three long ropes.

'Now we have to roll the trunk over the vines so we can tie them to it,' said Tom. He laid the ends of the vine ropes next to the ancient trunk. 'Push!' he ordered, putting his back against the wood.

Jamie did the same, but it didn't budge. Wanna lowered his bony head and shoved.

The tree trunk wobbled, then rolled over the vines.

'Thanks, Wanna!' Jamie said, knotting the vine ropes around it.

Tom took the other ends of the vine ropes and carefully carried them round to the

opposite side of the pit. He beckoned to
Jamie and Wanna to join him.

'I hope this works,' Jamie
murmured, as Tom handed a
rope to him and one to
Wanna, who clamped
it in his jaws.

'Take up the slack,' Tom told his friends.
'Get ready. Three, two, one . . . Pull!' They
each yanked on their vine rope. There was

a scrunching sliding noise as the tree trunk tipped into the pit, followed by a thump as it hit the bottom. Immediately they heard the scrabbling noise of claws on bark.

'The anteo's climbing out. Run!' Jamie yelled.

The boys and Wanna dropped the vines and raced away as fast as their legs would carry them, leaping over ferns and pushing through the jungle creepers. They didn't pause for breath until they were back at the gritty red sand and dusty rocks at the base of the mountain.

'We did it,' Tom gasped, bending over.

'We've never been eaten yet,' Jamie panted, grinning.

Gak!

Wanna bobbed his head up and down.

'Wanna agrees,' Tom laughed.

Gak! Gak! Gak!

Wanna's head was bobbing up and down so hard his scales were shaking.

The boys looked at each other.

'He's not agreeing—he's sounding the alarm,' Jamie said.

Eooowww!

The three of them froze. The bone-chilling cry was unmistakably the sound of the hunting anteo. It shrieked again, closer now.

'It's tracking us,' Tom whispered.

As quietly as they could, they scrambled towards the giant red boulders that surrounded the entrance to the underground cavern.

Behind them, they could hear the scritch-scratching of claws on stone. Jamie turned to see the anteo's bright green snout poke

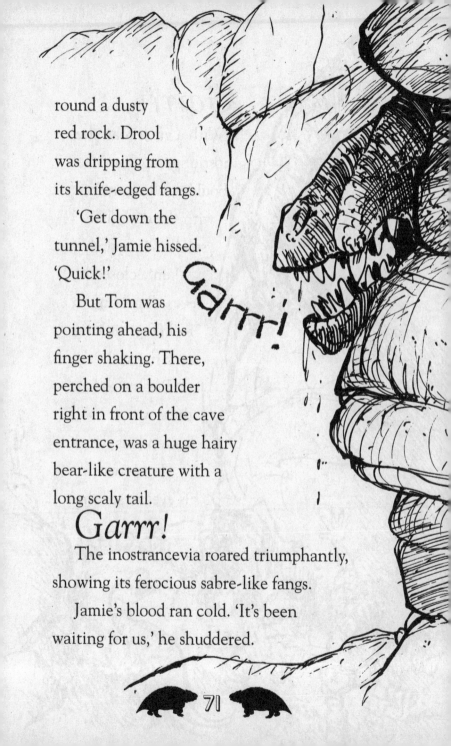

round a dusty
red rock. Drool
was dripping from
its knife-edged fangs.

'Get down the
tunnel,' Jamie hissed.
'Quick!'

But Tom was
pointing ahead, his
finger shaking. There,
perched on a boulder
right in front of the cave
entrance, was a huge hairy
bear-like creature with a
long scaly tail.

Garrr!

The inostrancevia roared triumphantly,
showing its ferocious sabre-like fangs.

Jamie's blood ran cold. 'It's been
waiting for us,' he shuddered.

Garrr!

With a great roar, the inostie sprang from the boulder, filling the air with the dung-like smell of its mangy fur.

Jamie closed his eyes, expecting to feel fangs sinking into his neck.

But instead there was a horrendous shriek. He opened his eyes to see the

Eooowww!

Garrr!

inostie attacking the anteosaurus. It jumped
onto the anteo's back and clawed at its side.
The anteo shook off the inostie and lunged
at its neck.

Jamie, Tom, and Wanna ducked behind
a boulder to watch the battle. Each creature
gave a terrible roar that echoed round the
mountainside. Then suddenly, the ferocious

predators turned away
from each other. The inostie
scrambled back up the mountain
and the anteo stalked back
towards the jungle.

'Time to make our getaway
too,' Jamie said.

The boys and Wanna lowered
themselves into the tunnel. The
little dino wagged his tail and
bounded off into the darkness.

'There he goes, back to the
Cretaceous to find some gingkoes
for his lunch,' Tom chuckled.

'It's time we went home for
lunch, too,' Jamie grinned, fitting
his foot into the first of the line
of dinosaur footprints
across the floor
of the cave.

Ahoy there

He stepped backwards into the print behind it, and in a flash, he was in the secret cave in Dinosaur Cove. A moment later, Tom was standing beside him.

'Ahoy there, me hearties,' Grandad greeted them as they walked back along the beach towards the old lighthouse. 'How did you get on with Pippin?'

'Oh—fine!' Jamie and Tom said together.

Grandad pointed to the shredded tartan blanket hanging out of Jamie's backpack. 'Looks like you had a bit of trouble,' he said.

One dangerous pit, two fearsome predators, and snowshoes for a pareiasaurus! Jamie thought. 'Just a bit,' he agreed, smiling at Tom.

DINOSAUR WORLD

- - - - BOYS' ROUTE

Mountains

Volcano

Underground cave

Jungle

Permian
Sea

Desert

Pools of Water

Swamp

Forest

Permian Sea

77

GLOSSARY

Anteosaurus (ant-ay-oh-sor-us) – a crocodile-like reptile that lived on land and in water. It had a thick head that it used to head-butt its enemies.

Cycads (si-kads) – plants with thick trunks, palm-like leaves and cones.

Gingko (gink-oh) – a tree native to China called a 'living fossil' because fossils of it have been found dating back millions of years, yet they are still around today. Also known as the stink bomb tree because of its smelly apricot-like fruit.

Inostrancevia (in-os-tran-see-vee-ah) – a large, predatory mammal-like reptile.

Pareiasaurus (par-ee-ah-sor-us) – a stocky, herbivorous reptile with bony skin and knobs on its skull. Some scientists think it might have evolved into a modern-day turtle.

Permian (per-mee-an) – the Permian period lasted from 290 to 248 million years ago. During this time the supercontinent Pangaea was formed and non-dinosaur reptiles roamed the earth.

Trilobite (try-loh-byt) – an extinct marine animal that had an outside skeleton divided into three parts.

Wannanosaurus (wah-nan-oh-sor-us) – a dinosaur that only ate plants and used its hard, flat skull to defend itself. Named after the place it was discovered: Wannano in China.

When we're angry

. . . keep out of our way!